The Complete
BRAMBLY HEDGE

For more information visit the Brambly Hedge website at:
www.bramblyhedge.com

This volume first published in Great Britain by HarperCollins Publishers Ltd in 1999
New edition published 2011

17

ISBN: 978-0-00-745016-9

Visit our website at: www.harpercollins.co.uk

Printed in China

The Complete
BRAMBLY HEDGE

JILL BARKLEM

HarperCollins *Children's Books*

Contents

INTRODUCTION

I am often asked how Brambly Hedge began and I find it hard to reply, for it seems to me that Brambly Hedge has always been there and my task has just been to make it visible.

Brambly Hedge is my ideal world. The way the mice live is completely natural, which is how I think life ought to be. They appreciate and use everything that grows around them. Theirs is a loving and caring society, but the mice are not just serious and worthy. They have FUN! Life is a series of picnics and gatherings, parties and outings.

It all began in March 1978 when I took my ideas into HarperCollins and met Jane Fior, who was to become my editor. She instantly saw what I was trying to do, and over the years she has helped me to organise this vision into a series of books for children. As we talked, all sorts of stories began to spring to mind.

I began to write about and to draw Brambly Hedge. Inevitably, the pictures always fell short of what I could see in my mind's eye. To capture what I see on paper is like catching a butterfly – just when I think I have it, it flits off again.

I planned to do four books about spring, summer, autumn and winter and so I immersed myself in each season as it came round. I researched all the time, filling notebooks and files with every possible detail of a mouse's life. As far as possible, I had to eliminate human concepts. For example, I worked out a system of measurement based on tails and paws rather than feet and inches. Weight is measured with acorns and grains of wheat and time is measured with sundials, candle clocks and water clocks.

The first four books were published in 1980. I then decided to explore the world beyond Brambly Hedge, to go deeper into the places we can glimpse in the pictures. And I also wanted to bring a new generation of mice to the hedge. The first of these stories, *The Secret Staircase*, came about as I told my daughter Lizzie a bedtime story. She was far too young to understand the details but she loved to hear about the little mice who climbed the stairs to find a secret playroom. Later came *The High Hills, Sea Story* and then *Poppy's Babies.*

Creating the books is tremendous fun, but very hard work at the same time. This is because I like to get everything right. Each flower must have the correct number of petals and be growing in the right place, at the right time. Everything the mice make or do must be possible for them, living where they do. After all, Brambly Hedge is real, and I am simply here to record it.

Jill Barklem

SPRING STORY

It was the most beautiful morning. The spring sunshine crept into every cottage along Brambly Hedge and the little windows in the trees were opened wide.

All the mice were up early, but earliest of all was Wilfred, who lived with his family in the hornbeam tree. It was Wilfred's birthday.

Jumping out of bed, he ran into his parents' room and bounced on their bed till they gave him their presents.

"Happy birthday, Wilfred," said Mr and Mrs Toadflax sleepily.

He tore off the pretty wrappings and scattered them all over the floor. His squeaks of excitement woke his brother and sisters.

His parents turned over to go to sleep again. Wilfred went and sat on the stairs and blew his new whistle.

Mr and Mrs Apple lived next door at Crabapple Cottage. The sound of Wilfred's whistle floated in through their bedroom window. Mrs Apple got up and stretched. She sniffed the sweet air and went down to the kitchen to make a pot of elderflower tea. She was a very kindly mouse and a wonderful cook. The cottage always smelled of newly-made bread, fresh cakes and blackberry puddings.

"Breakfast's ready," she called. Mr Apple got out of bed with a sigh and joined her at the kitchen table. They ate their toast and jam and listened to Wilfred's warbling.

"I think somebody needs a lesson from the blackbird," said Mr Apple, brushing the crumbs from his whiskers and putting on his coat.

Mr Apple was a nice, old-fashioned sort of mouse. He was warden of the Store Stump where all the food for Brambly Hedge was kept.

The Store Stump was not far away. As Mr Apple
walked happily through the grass to the big front doors,
he felt someone pull his tail. He turned around quickly.
It was Wilfred, whistle in hand.

"It's my birthday!" he squeaked.

"Is it, young mouse," said Mr Apple. "Happy birthday to you! Would you like to come and help me check the Store Stump? We'll see what we can find."

In the middle of the Stump was an enormous hall, and leading off from it many passages and staircases. These led in turn to dozens of storerooms full of nuts and honey and jams and pickles. Each one had to be inspected. Wilfred's legs felt tired by the time they had finished and he sat by the fire in the hall to rest. Mr Apple lifted down a jar of sugared violets. He made a little cornet from a twist of paper and filled it with sweets. Taking Wilfred by the paw, he led him through the dark corridors out into the sun. Wilfred went to look for his brother and Mr Apple hurried down the hedge to visit his daughter Daisy and her husband, Lord Woodmouse.

Lord and Lady Woodmouse lived in the Old Oak Palace in the middle of the hedge. From the outside, the Palace looked like an ordinary oak tree, but inside the trunk was hollowed out to form a beautiful and many-roomed mansion.

At its heart was the grand ballroom. Polished doors led to magnificent kitchens, dining rooms, bedrooms, playrooms, spiral staircases and secret passages. Old Oak Palace had always been the home of the Woodmouse family.

Upstairs in the best bedroom, Lord and Lady Woodmouse
woke to bright sunshine.

"What a perfect day!" sighed Lady Daisy as she nibbled
a primrose biscuit. When they heard that Daisy's father had
come to call, they were soon up and dressed and
running down the winding stairs to greet him.

They found him in the kitchen drinking mint tea with Mrs Crustybread, the Palace cook. Daisy gave Mr Apple a kiss and sat down beside him.

"Hello Papa," she said. "What brings you here so early?"

"I've just met little Wilfred – it's his birthday today. Shall we arrange a surprise picnic for him?"

"What a wonderful idea," said Lord Woodmouse. Daisy nodded.

"I'll make him a special birthday cake if his mother agrees," said Mrs Crustybread, hurrying off to the pantry to find the ingredients.

Everyone was to be invited of course, so Mr Apple set off up the hedge towards the woods and Lord Woodmouse went down towards the stream calling at each house on the way.

The first house on Mr Apple's route was Elderberry Lodge. This fine elder bush was Basil's home. Basil was in charge of the Store Stump cellars. He was just getting up.

"A picnic eh? Splendid! I'll bring up some rose petal wine," he said, shuffling absent-mindedly round the room looking for his trousers. Basil had long white whiskers and always wore a scarlet waistcoat. He used to keep the other mice amused for hours with his stories.

"Ah, there you are, you rascals," he exclaimed, discovering his trousers behind the sofa.

Next Mr Apple came to the hornbeam. Mr Toadflax was sitting on his front doorstep eating bread and bramble jelly.

"We thought it would be nice to have a surprise picnic for your Wilfred," whispered Mr Apple. "We won't tell him what it's for and we'll all meet at midday by the Palace roots."

Mr Toadflax was delighted with the suggestion and went inside to tell his wife. Mr Apple went on to visit Old Vole who lived in a tussock of grass in the middle of the field.

Lord Woodmouse, meanwhile, was working his way
down to the stream. The news had travelled ahead of
him and all along the hedge excited mice leaned out of
their windows to ask when the picnic would take place.

"I'll see if I can find some preserves," said old
Mrs Eyebright.

"Shall we bring tablecloths?" called the weavers
who lived in the tangly hawthorn trees.

Poppy Eyebright from
the dairy promised cheeses,

and Dusty Dogwood, the Miller,
offered a batch of buns.

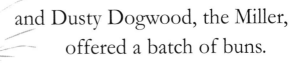

Mice soon began calling at the Store Stump to collect clover flour and honey, bramble brandy and poppy seeds, and all the other good things needed for the picnic. Mrs Crustybread baked a huge hazelnut cake with layers of thick cream and Wilfred's mother decorated it. Mrs Apple made some of her special primrose puddings.

Wilfred knew that there was to be an outing and that if he behaved, he would be allowed to go. He did his best but with a new whistle, a drum and a peashooter for his birthday, it wasn't easy.

When the Toadflax family arrived at the Palace,
Wilfred was rather disappointed that no one there
seemed to know that it was his birthday. Indeed he
had rather hoped for a few more presents, but it

would have been rude to drop hints, so he hid
his feelings as best he could. At a signal from
Lord Woodmouse they all set off with their baskets,
hampers and wheelbarrows.

Everyone had something to carry. Wilfred was given an enormous basket, so heavy he could hardly lift it. Mr Apple lent him a wheelbarrow, and his brother and sisters helped him to push it, but still poor Wilfred found it hard to keep up.

It was a very long way. Heaving and pulling, wheeling and hauling, the mice made their way round the Palace, through the cornfield and up by the stream. Wilfred felt very hot and he wanted a rest.

"Here we are!" cried Lord Woodmouse at last.

The baskets were put down and opened, and nettlestem cloths spread out on the mossy grass. In no time at all, the food was unpacked. Wilfred was exhausted. He sat on his basket, too tired to open it, his whiskers drooping sadly.

Mr Apple said grace: "For this good food from our green fields, may we be very grateful."

"I think the knives are in your basket, Wilfred," said Mrs Apple kindly. "If you get them out, we can cut the pies."

Slowly, Wilfred slipped from his perch and undid the catch. When he lifted the lid, he could hardly believe his eyes.

Inside the hamper, packed all around with presents, was an enormous cake, and on the top, written in pink icing, was HAPPY BIRTHDAY WILFRED.

"Happy Birthday, dear Wilfred,
Happy Birthday to you," sang the mice.

When Wilfred had opened all his presents, Basil said,
"Give us a tune," so he bashfully stood up and played
Hickory, Dickory, Dandelion Clock on his new whistle.
Mrs Toadflax nudged him meaningfully when he
had finished.

"Er . . . thank you for all my lovely presents,"
said Wilfred, trying to avoid Mrs Crustybread's eye.
She had caught him firing acorns through
her kitchen window earlier in the day.

"Now for tea," announced Daisy Woodmouse.

The mice sat on the grass and Wilfred handed round the cake.

When tea was over, the grown-ups snoozed under the bluebells, while the young mice played hide-and-seek in the primroses.

At last the sun began to sink behind the Far Woods and a chilly breeze blew over the field. It was time to go home.

When the moon came up that night, Brambly Hedge was silent and still. Every mouse was fast asleep.

SUMMER STORY

It was a very hot summer.

Each day the sun rose high in the blue sky and the fields shimmered in the heat.

The hedgerow was quiet. Many of the mice preferred to stay inside their shady cottages, trying to keep cool.

Out of doors, the best place to be was down by the stream. The mice gathered there in the afternoon, sat under the bank in the shade, and dangled their paws and tails in the clear water.

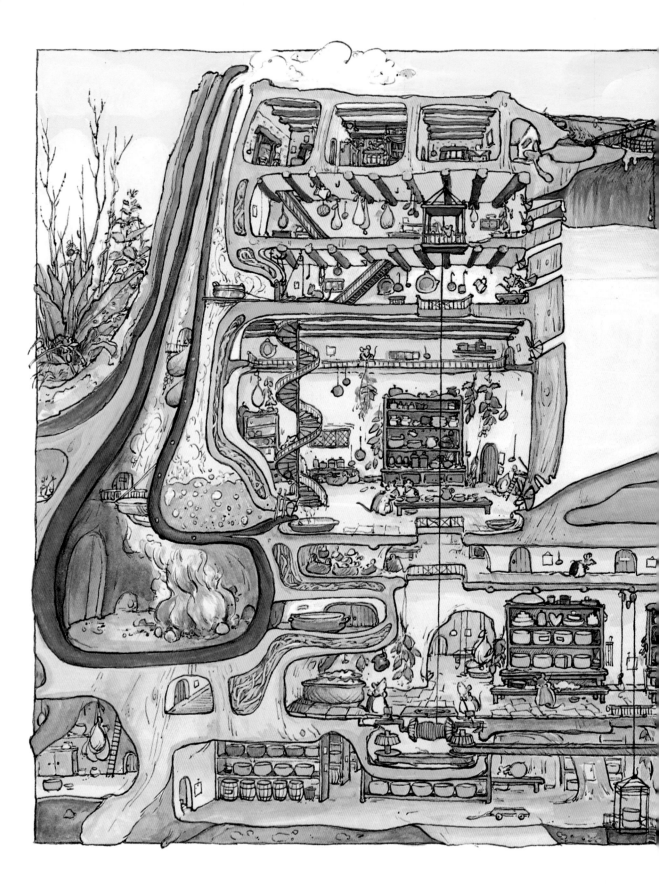

On the banks of the stream were the flour and dairy mills. The flow of the water turned the wheels which ground the flour and churned the butter for Brambly Hedge.

Poppy Eyebright looked after the Dairy Stump. She supervised the large vat into which milk, kindly given by some friendly cows, was poured and stored. The many kitchens, where cheeses were drained and shaped, smoked and wrapped, were also in her care.

Poppy was not fond of hot weather. Her pats of butter began to melt unless they were wrapped in cool dock leaves, and the pots of cream had to be hung in the millpool to keep them fresh.

When her work was finished she would wander out by the millwheel, enjoying the splashes of cool water.

The flour mill, further down the stream, was run by the miller, Dusty Dogwood. Dogwood was his family name, but he was called Dusty because he was always covered from tail to whiskers with flour dust.

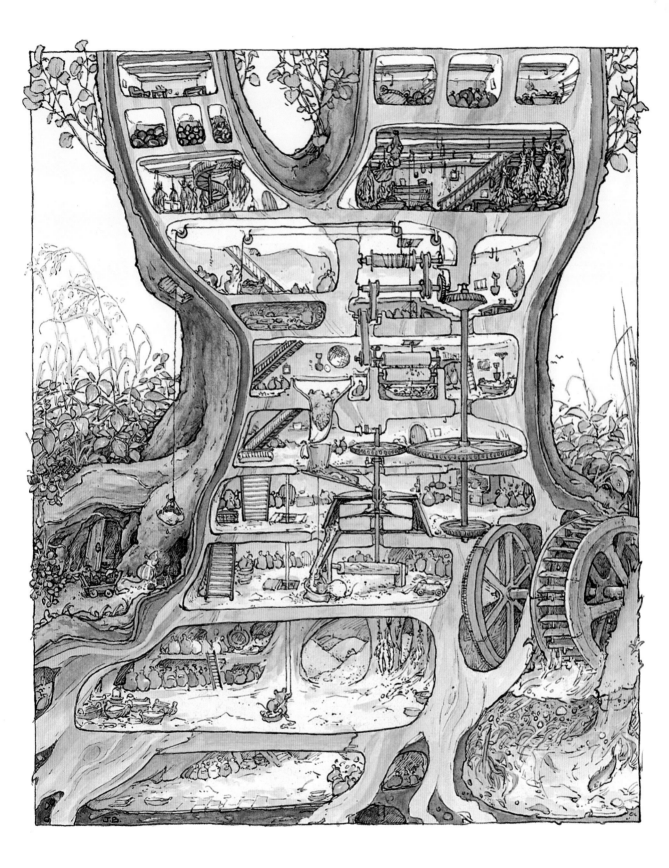

He was a cheerful and friendly mouse, like his father, his grandfather, and his great-grandfather, who had all run the mill before him. He loved the fine weather and strolled up and down the stream, chatting to the paddlers and dabblers.

His walks took him past the Dairy, where he would often see Poppy standing by the stream, looking very pretty. As the long, hot days went by, Dusty used to spend more and more time walking up to the Dairy, and Poppy used to go out more and more often to the mossy shadows of the millwheel…

Early in June, Miss Poppy Eyebright and Mr Dusty Dogwood officially announced their engagement. Everyone along the hedgerow was delighted.

Midsummer's Day was picked for the wedding and preparations were started at once. Poppy was so sure the weather would hold that they decided the wedding should take place on the stream. It was the coolest place, and besides, it was very romantic.

Dusty found a large, flat piece of bark up in the woods, which a party of mice carried down to the water's edge. It was floated, with some difficulty, just under the mill weir, and tethered in midstream by plaited rush and nettle ropes.

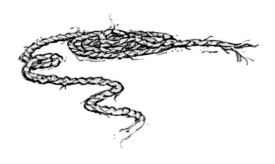

Poppy prepared her trousseau. Every afternoon
she sat in the shade of some tall kingcups embroidering
her wedding dress, which she hid as soon as she saw
anyone coming along the path.

The wedding day dawned at last. The sky was clear
and blue and it was hotter than ever. The kitchens
of Brambly Hedge were full of activity. Cool summer
foods were being made. There was cold watercress
soup, fresh dandelion salad, honey creams, syllabubs
and meringues.

The young mice had been up early to gather huge baskets of wild strawberries.

Basil selected some white wines, primrose, meadowsweet and elderflower, and hung them to cool in the rushes. Basil was in charge of all the cellars under the Store Stump. He was a stout, good-natured mouse, with long white whiskers and a sensitive nose for fine wine.

In her rooms above the Dairy, Poppy dressed carefully. She polished her whiskers and dabbed rosewater behind her ears. Her straw bonnet, which Lady Woodmouse had trimmed with flowers, hung from the bedpost, and her bridal posy lay waiting on the windowsill. She peeped at her reflection in the shiny wardrobe door, took a deep breath, and ran downstairs to join her bridesmaids.

Dusty kept his best suit in a basket under the stairs to protect it from the moths. He put it on and tucked a daisy in his buttonhole. "I'd better just check that barley I ground yesterday," he said to himself. He ran up the steps at such a pace that the whole mill seemed to shake. The wooden floor above him let down a cloud of dust, all over his new wedding suit.

"Bother it!" he said, sitting on a sack of corn and looking at his mottled jacket in dismay.

There was a thumping on the door below and his friend Conker called through the letterbox, "Dusty, are you ready? It's nearly time to go."

Dusty sighed and went morosely down the stairs.

As soon as Conker saw him, he began to giggle.

"Dusty by name, dusty by nature," he said, trying to remedy matters with his clean handkerchief.

The floury dust swirled and settled again on whiskers, tails, best clothes and buttonholes. The two mice looked at each other and started to laugh. They laughed so much that they had to sit down on a flour bag to recover.

The wedding was to take place at midday and Dusty and Conker arrived just in time. The guests were all in their finest clothes. Three young mice, dressed in smart blue suits, had been chosen as pages and were busily directing everyone to their places. Mrs Apple discreetly tried to dust down the groom and best man, but to little avail.

At last old Mrs Eyebright, Poppy's grandmother, spotted the bride and her little bridesmaids coming through the grass. The pages squeaked with excitement and got into place. Every head turned to watch the bride as she made her way through the buttercups and stepped onto the decorated raft.

The Old Vole, who had been asked to perform the ceremony, stood up and said in a kindly voice:

"Poppy Eyebright, do you love Dusty Dogwood and will you love him and care for him for ever

and ever?" Poppy vowed that she would.

"Dusty Dogwood, do you love Poppy and will you love her and look after her for ever and ever?"

"I will," said Dusty. Mrs Apple blew her nose.

"Then in the name of the flowers and the fields, the stars in the sky, and the streams that flow down to the sea, and the mystery that breathes wonder into all these things, I pronounce you mouse and wife." All the mice cheered as Dusty kissed his bride,

and the bridesmaids threw baskets of petals over the happy couple. Mrs Apple wiped a tear from her eye and the dancing and feasting began.

First they danced, for no one could keep still, jigs, reels and quadrilles.

Mr Apple proposed a toast.

"To the bride and groom! May their tails grow long, and their eyes be bright, and all their squeaks be little ones."

The guests raised their glasses and then they danced again. The dancing was so vigorous that the raft bobbed up and down. Gradually the ropes holding the raft began to wear through.

One by one, the little ropes snapped, until finally the very last one gave way.

They were carried into midstream by the current.
The young mice squeaked with alarm at first, but
as they seemed to come to no harm, they continued
with the feast.

The raft floated gently past fields of buttercups and meadowsweet, and the voles tending the fires in the Pottery came out to wave as the wedding party drifted by.

Eventually, the raft was caught in a
leafy clump of rushes and forget-me-nots.
The ropes were made fast and the dancing
began again.

At last the dusk came, golden and misty over the
fields. The blue sky slowly darkened and the mice
began to think about getting home. All the food was
finished up and the pots and pans hidden in the
rushes to be collected the next day.

They walked back through the fields in the evening
sun, looking very splendid in their wedding clothes.
The Old Vole was taken back to his hole first and the
rest of the mice gradually made their way home to
bed, exhausted but happy.

And what happened to Poppy and Dusty?

They slipped quietly away to the primrose woods. The primroses were over, but there, hidden amongst the long grass and ferns, wild roses and honeysuckle, was the cottage in which they had chosen to stay.

It was the perfect place for a honeymoon.

AUTUMN STORY

It was a fine autumn. The blackberries were ripe, and the nuts were ready, and the mice of Brambly Hedge were very busy. Every morning they went out into the fields to gather seeds, berries and roots, which they took back to the Store Stump and carefully stowed away for the winter ahead. The Store Stump was warm inside and smelled deliciously of bramble jelly and rising bread, and it was already nearly full of food.

Lord Woodmouse, who lived in the Old Oak Palace, was out early with his youngest daughter, Primrose.

"Now keep close to me, and don't get lost," he said, as they made their way along the blackberry bushes. Primrose picked the berries nearest the ground while her father hooked the upper branches down with his walking stick.

The basket was nearly full when they were joined by old Mrs Eyebright.

"I've been looking for you," she said. "Bad weather's on its way, I can feel it in my bones. We must finish our harvesting before the rain begins."

Lord Woodmouse sent Primrose back to the Palace and then went on to the Store Stump to find Mr Apple to make arrangements. Soon parties of mice with carts and wheelbarrows were hurrying out to the fields to gather the last of the nuts and berries.

Lord and Lady Woodmouse decided to help
pick mushrooms and they were just setting
off when Lady Woodmouse cried out in alarm,
"Where's Primrose?"

She was nowhere to be seen.

She wasn't hiding in the baskets, or under the leaves,
or in the long grass.

"Has anyone seen Primrose?" shouted Lord Woodmouse.

"She hasn't been here," replied the mice gathering berries
high in the blackthorn bush.

"We haven't seen her," called the mice in the tangly
hawthorn trees.

The children thought she was at her grandmother's house and a search party was sent along to investigate.

Hot and out of breath, they knocked at the door of Crabapple Cottage.

"Have you seen Primrose?" asked Wilfred. "We've lost her."

Mrs Apple shook her head, took off her apron, and joined in the search. Mr Apple ran over to the gap in the hedge by the Store Stump.

"Primrose, where are you?" he cried.

"Primrose, where are you?" echoed the call across the cornfield.

Lord and Lady Woodmouse went back to the Palace.
They looked in the cupboards and under the beds.
The Store Stump was searched from top to bottom.
"Oh dear!" said Lady Daisy.
"She's such a little mouse.
Where can she be?
What shall we do?"

Meanwhile, Primrose, wandering along the edge of the cornfield, was quite unaware of her parents' concern. She had spent the morning picking wild flowers and gazing up at the blue sky, and after a lunch of blackberries, she had dozed a little in the sun. She was just going to help a group of mice she had seen gathering seeds in the ditch, when she spotted a little round house high up in the stalks of the corn.

"I wonder who lives there," she thought, and decided to climb up and peep through one of the windows.

As she looked in, she saw two pairs of bright little eyes peering back at her.

"I – I do beg your pardon," she stammered, and began to climb down again.

"We were just going to have tea," a voice called after her, "Won't you join us?"

Primrose found the tiny front door and went inside. It was very cosy. There was a thistledown carpet on the floor and the neatly-woven grass walls were covered with books and pictures. The two elderly harvest mice who lived in the house were very glad to have a visitor. They sat Primrose down, gave her a slice of cake and handed her their album of family portraits to look at.

When Primrose had been shown all their treasures, she thanked the mice politely and climbed down to the ground again. She decided to walk to the edge of the Chestnut Woods before she went home. Some Brambly Hedge mice were still there, picking blackberries in the last of the evening sun, but they were too busy to notice her. She peered into the grasses, looking for feathers and other useful things.

Hidden in the brambles, she discovered a very interesting hole.

"I wonder if anyone lives down there," she said to herself, and wandered into the tunnel.

It was very dark inside but she could just see round front doors set in the walls of the branching passages. As she went deeper into the tunnel, it became darker still and soon Primrose could see nothing at all.

"I don't think I like this place," said Primrose with a shiver, "I'm going home."

She turned to leave, but with so many passages leading this way and that, she had no idea which way she had come. She picked up her skirts and ran through the maze of tunnels.

At last she saw a glimmer of light and ran towards it. The passage opened into a thick clump of brambles and briars under some tall trees. Primrose had no idea where she was.

"I can't see the oak tree," she said in a small voice, "and I can't see the willow by the stream. I think I must be lost."

It was getting very dark. Big drops of rain began to fall and splashed through the leaves around her. Primrose huddled under a toadstool and tried not to cry.

In the distance a lonely owl hooted and the branches of the trees above creaked in the rising wind. There were little scrabbling noises in the bush quite near to Primrose, and these worried her most of all.

It got darker and darker and soon everything disappeared into the night.

Primrose was just trying not to think about weasels, when to her horror she saw five little flickering lights coming through the woods towards her. She could just

make out five strange figures behind them. They were shapeless and bulgy and seemed to have no heads at all. Primrose wriggled further back into the brambles.

The figures came closer and closer and Primrose realised that they were going to pass right by her hiding place.

The nearer they came, the worse they looked, and she shut her eyes as she heard them pass only a whisker away from where she was sitting. One . . . two . . . three . . . four . . .

She decided to be very brave and take a peep at
the fifth as it went by.

It walked with a limp. It had a tail. And whiskers.
And Mr Apple's trousers.

"GRANDPA!" she squeaked with delight.

As each of the figures turned round she recognised them; Mr Apple, Mrs Apple, Dusty Dogwood and best of all, her own mother and father.

Primrose pushed her way through the brambles.

"Primrose!" cried Lady Daisy. "You're safe!"

"The harvest mice said you had gone to the woods, but it was so dark and wet that we'd almost given up hope of finding you," said her father, and he picked her up and wrapped her snugly in his cloak.

Primrose was nearly asleep by the time they got home. Lady Woodmouse carried her up to her little room and took off her wet clothes. A clean nightie was warming by the fire and a mug of hot acorn coffee had been placed by the bed.

"I'll never ever go out of the field on my own again," Primrose whispered sleepily.

Her mother gave her a kiss and smoothed her pillow.

"Ease your whiskers, rest your paws,
Pies and puddings fill the stores.
Sweetly dream the night away,
Till sunshine brings another day,"

. . . she sang softly, tucking Primrose into her comfy bed.

WINTER STORY

It was the middle of winter. The sun had just set
and it was very, very cold. An icy wind was blowing
from the East and the wind promised snow.
  Deep in the dark roots of Brambly Hedge tiny
lights appeared as lamps were lit in the windows.

More little lights could be seen leaving the Store
Stump, moving hastily along the hedgerow and
disappearing into holes hidden in the twisty roots.
The mice had smelled snow in the air and were
all hurrying home to a nice hot supper by the fire.

Mr Apple, warden of the Store Stump, was the last to leave for home. By the time he reached Crabapple Cottage, the first flakes were beginning to fall.

"Is that you, dear?" called Mrs Apple as he let himself in through the front door. Delicious smells wafted down from the kitchen. Mrs Apple had spent the afternoon baking pies, cakes and puddings for the cold days to come. She drew two armchairs up to the fire and brought in their supper on a tray.

There was a lot of noise coming from the hornbeam tree next door. The Toadflax children had never seen snow before.

"It's snowing! It really is SNOWING!" squeaked the two boys, Wilfred and Teasel. They chased their sisters

Clover and Catkin round the kitchen, with pawfuls of
snow scooped from the windowsill.

"Suppertime!" called Mrs Toadflax firmly, ladling hot
chestnut soup into four small bowls.

After supper the children were sent off to bed, but they were far too excited to sleep. As soon as the grown-ups were safely occupied downstairs, they climbed out of their bunk beds to watch the snowflakes falling past the window.

"Tobogganing tomorrow," said Wilfred.

"Snow pancakes for tea," said Clover.

"We'll make a snow mouse," said Catkin.

"And I'll knock it down!" said Teasel, pushing the girls off their chair.

Next morning the mice along the hedgerow woke to find their windows half-blocked by snow. Mrs Apple had to stand on tiptoes on the kitchen table to see out.

And what a sight met her eyes! The fields were covered with a thick, white blanket of snow and all the paths and plants had disappeared beneath it.

When the Toadflax family went down to breakfast, they found the kitchen dark and still. Mrs Toadflax put fresh wood on the fire and set Clover to work with the toasting fork. Soon they were all sitting round the table, eating hot buttered toast, drinking blackberry leaf tea and making plans for the day ahead.

The snow was thicker than the mice had expected. All the downstairs windows along the hedgerow were covered with snow and many of the upper ones, too, were hidden in deep drifts.

The mice leaned out of their bedroom windows to wave and call to their friends.

"Enough for a Snow Ball, wouldn't you say?" called Mr Toadflax to Mrs Apple.

"A Snow Ball!" echoed the little mice, gleefully.

Every family along the hedgerow kept shovels,
maps and ropes in a special cupboard by the front
door and after breakfast the mice dug tunnels from
tree to tree, linking them all to the Store Stump.
Teasel and Wilfred were sent down to help, but they
soon found that it was much more fun to throw snow
at each other and so were sent home again.

Lord Woodmouse dug his way through to old
Mrs Eyebright and helped her to light a fire.

"I haven't seen snow like this since I was young,"
she sighed. "The last Snow Ball was held in the
year Mr Eyebright and I were married. I'm the
only one left who can remember it now."

When the tunnels were finished, all the mice
gathered noisily in the Store Stump Hall.

Mrs Apple took some seed cake from the cupboard and prepared a jug of acorn coffee. The mice helped themselves and gathered round Mr Apple, who held up a paw for silence.

"Lord Woodmouse and I have agreed," he said when they were quiet, "that we should follow in the tradition of our forefathers." He cleared his throat nervously, straightened his whiskers, and recited,

"When the snows are lying deep,
When the field has gone to sleep,
When the blackthorn turns to white,
And frosty stars bejewel the night,
When summer streams are turned to ice,
A Snow Ball warms the hearts of mice.

"Friends, I declare that a Snow Ball will take place at dusk tonight in the Ice Hall."

"Where's that?" whispered Clover, as the mice clapped and cheered.

"Wait and see!" replied Mrs Apple. "You come home with me and help prepare the feast."

There was a deep drift of snow banked against the Store Stump and the elder mice, after discussion, declared it to be "just right" for the Ice Hall. Mr Apple dug the first tunnel to check that the snow was firm.

"It's perfect!" he called back from the middle of the drift. The mice picked up their shovels and the digging began.

The snow was dug from inside the drift, piled into carts and taken down to the stream. Wilfred and Teasel helped enthusiastically, but they were sent home again when Mr Apple caught them putting icicles down Catkin's dress.

The middle of the drift was carefully hollowed out. Mr Apple inspected the roof very thoroughly to make sure that it was safe.

"Safe as the Store Stump!" he declared.

All the kitchens along Brambly Hedge were
warm and busy. Hot soups, punches and puddings
bubbled and in the ovens pies browned and sizzled.
Clover and Catkin helped Mrs Apple string

There was a deep drift of snow banked against the Store Stump and the elder mice, after discussion, declared it to be "just right" for the Ice Hall. Mr Apple dug the first tunnel to check that the snow was firm.

"It's perfect!" he called back from the middle of the drift. The mice picked up their shovels and the digging began.

The snow was dug from inside the drift, piled into carts and taken down to the stream. Wilfred and Teasel helped enthusiastically, but they were sent home again when Mr Apple caught them putting icicles down Catkin's dress.

The middle of the drift was carefully hollowed out. Mr Apple inspected the roof very thoroughly to make sure that it was safe.

"Safe as the Store Stump!" he declared.

All the kitchens along Brambly Hedge were
warm and busy. Hot soups, punches and puddings
bubbled and in the ovens pies browned and sizzled.
Clover and Catkin helped Mrs Apple string

crabapples to roast over the fire. The boys had
to sit and watch because they ate too many.

"It's not that I mind, dears, but we must have SOME
left for the punch!"

The Glow-worms were put in charge of the lighting. Mr Toadflax fetched them early from the bank at the end of the Hedge, for Mrs Apple had insisted that they should have a good supper before their long night's work began.

By tea-time the Hall was finished. The ice columns and carvings sparkled in the blue-green light and the polished dance floor shone. Tables were set at the end of the Hall and eager cooks bustled in from their kitchens with baskets of food.

The children decorated a small raised platform with sprays of holly, while Basil, the keeper of the hedgerow wines, set out some chairs for the musicians.

When all was done, the mice admired their handiwork and went home to wash and change.

As muffs and mufflers were left at the door, it was clear that all the mice had dressed up for the grand occasion. Wilfred and Teasel crept under a table to watch and every now and then a little paw appeared and a cream cake disappeared.

Basil struck up a jolly tune on his violin and the
dancing began. All the dances were very fast and twirly
and were made even faster by the slippery ice floor.
Wilfred and Teasel whirled their sisters round so quickly
that their paws left the ground.

"I don't feel very well," said Clover, looking rather green.

Mrs Apple stood on a chair and banged two saucepan lids together.

"Supper is served," she called.

The eating and drinking and dancing carried on late into the night. At midnight, all the hedgerow children were taken home to bed.

As soon as they were safely tucked up, their parents returned to the Ball. Basil made some hot blackberry punch and the dancing got faster and faster.

The Snow Ball went on until dawn.

The musicians were tired. The ice columns began to drip. The sleepy mice could dance no more. They wandered home through the snow tunnels, climbed the stairs and crept into their warm beds.

Outside the window, the snow had started to fall again. But every mouse in Brambly Hedge was fast asleep.

THE
SECRET
STAIRCASE

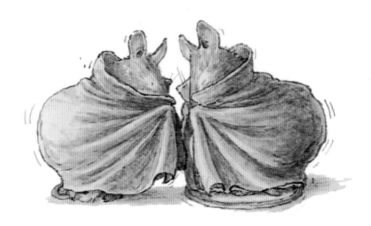

It was a frosty morning. The air was crisp and cold and everything sparkled in the winter sunshine. The little mice hurrying along the path turned up their collars and blew on their paws in an effort to keep warm.

"Merry Midwinter," panted Dusty Dogwood, scurrying past Mr Apple and the Toadflax children with a huge

covered basket. Mr Apple and the children were busy
too, dragging great sprays of holly and trails of ivy
and mistletoe towards the Old Oak Palace. When they
arrived at the gates, they heaped all the branches on
the ground and Wilfred tugged on the bell.

Lord Woodmouse and Primrose, his daughter, opened the door.

"Here we are," said Mr Apple, mopping his face, "do you want it all inside?"

"Yes, please," said Lord Woodmouse. "We'll start by decorating the stairs." Eagerly, the children pulled the branches over the polished palace floors and skidded their way into the Great Hall.

"Are you two ready for tonight?" asked Lord Woodmouse.

Primrose and Wilfred exchanged glances. That evening, after dark, all the mice would gather round a blazing fire for the traditional midwinter celebrations. A grand entertainment was planned and Primrose and Wilfred had chosen to give a recitation.

"Almost," said Primrose, "but we've still got to practise and we need proper costumes."

"You'd better see your mother about those," replied her father. "You can practise wherever you like."

Leaving Clover, Catkin and Teasel to go back to the wood with Mr Apple, Primrose and Wilfred took themselves off to a corner of the hall and began to go through their lines.

"*When the days are the shortest, the nights are the coldest...*" began Primrose, drawing an imaginary cloak around her.

"*The frost is the sharpest, the year is the oldest...*" continued Wilfred.

"Look out, you two," interrupted Basil, bustling past with some bottles.

"This is hopeless," sighed Primrose. "We can't rehearse here. Let's go and ask Mama what to do."

Lady Woodmouse was busy making caraway biscuits
in the kitchen. She leaned on her rolling pin to listen
to Primrose's tale of woe.

"Why don't you see if there's something up in the
attics for you to wear," she said. "You could practise
up there too." She packed a little basket with bread and
cheese and a jug of blackberry juice and shooed the
children gently out of the kitchen.

There were a great many attic rooms at the top of Old Oak Palace. Lady Woodmouse used them to tidy away things that might come in useful. Babies' blankets and rolls of lace, boxes of buttons, stacks of books, broken toys, patchwork quilts, pudding cloths and old saucepans were all crammed together, higgledy-piggledy, on the shelves.

Primrose and Wilfred went from room to room looking for a suitable spot for their rehearsal. They ended up in a crowded storeroom at the end of a passage, but it was difficult to concentrate on practising, there were so many things to look at.

Standing on tiptoe, Primrose reached inside the drawer of an old wooden dresser. In it, she found some bundles of letters tied up in pink ribbon but she couldn't read the writing and as it's rude to read other people's letters, she put them back. As she did so, she caught sight of a small key which had slipped down at the side of the drawer.

"Look at this, Wilfred," she cried excitedly.

"Let's see. Oh, it's only an old key," said Wilfred. "Is it time for lunch?"

Primrose said nothing, but she slipped the key into her pinafore pocket before setting out their picnic on the floor.

"Do you think this would make a cloak?" said Wilfred, his mouth full of bread and cheese. He had seized the end of a long green curtain and was winding himself up in it. As he turned towards Primrose, he caught sight of a small door hidden behind its folds.

"Where does this go to, Primrose?" he asked.

"I don't know," replied Primrose, scrambling over some boxes. "Does it open?"

Wilfred pushed. The door was locked. He peeped through the keyhole and saw another flight of stairs on the other side of the door.

"It's no good," he said, disappointedly, "we can't get in."

"If there's a keyhole, there must be a key," said Primrose, "and I think I have it here!" She reached inside her pinafore pocket and handed the little key to Wilfred. He tried it in the lock. It fitted perfectly and the door swung open.

They found themselves in a dark panelled hall at the foot of a long winding staircase. The stair carpet must once have been beautiful, but now it was tattered and covered with dust.

"No one can have been up here for years and years," whispered Primrose. "Shall we see what's at the top?"

Wilfred nodded, so up the stairs they went, round and round. Primrose kept close behind Wilfred, she couldn't help feeling a little nervous. Suddenly the stairs came to an abrupt end. They were standing in yet another hall, and there ahead was yet another door, but this time it was huge and richly carved. They went up to it and Wilfred gave it a push. As the door opened, the children stared about them in amazement.

They were standing in the most magnificent room. There were columns and carvings, and dark tapestries and paintings on the walls. In front of them two golden chairs stood on a little platform. Everything in the room was covered in dust and the air smelled musty and strange.

"Where are we?" asked Wilfred.

"I don't know," whispered Primrose. "I've never been here before."

They tiptoed across the floor, leaving footprints as they went.

"Maybe your ancestors lived here in the olden days, Primrose," said Wilfred, gazing at an imposing portrait.

"Let's clean it all up and have it as our house," said Primrose. "We could keep it secret and come up here to play."

As she spoke, she opened a cupboard and found it full of hats.

"Wilfred! Look at these. They're just right for tonight!"

A door at the end of the room led into a nursery. There was a canopied cot near the window, and all sorts of dust-covered toys were on the shelves.

Wilfred peered inside an ancient trunk and pulled out a little suit with a high jacket and tight braided trousers. It was almost the right size for him. Neatly folded beneath it were dresses and cloaks, waistcoats and shawls, some trimmed with gold and others studded with shining stones. The children held them up, one after another, and each chose an outfit for the evening and tried it on.

"Perfect! And now we must practise."

"Let's finish exploring first," said Wilfred.

They seemed to be in a whole suite of rooms. There was a dining room, a butler's pantry, a small kitchen and several other bedrooms. The bathroom was particularly grand with a tiled floor and high windows. Wilfred rubbed a mirror clean and made faces at himself whilst Primrose leaned over the side of the bath to try the taps. No water came out.

"*When the days are the shortest, the nights are the coldest…*" she recited. Her voice sounded loud and echoey. Wilfred joined in, and they went through their lines again and again until they were word-perfect.

Outside the red sun was sinking low in the frosty air, and the bathroom was filled with shadows.

"It's getting late," said Primrose. "If we don't hurry, we'll miss the log."

They picked up their clothes and scampered over the dusty floors to the door.

Down the stairs they ran, round and round, down
and down, till they found themselves back in the
storeroom. They locked the door with the little key

and replaced it in the drawer. Then they crept along the corridors to Primrose's room, taking care to keep out of sight.

Primrose opened her window. They could just hear the carolling of the mice as the midwinter log was pulled along the hedge. There was no time to change, so they threw on their cloaks to hide their costumes and ran to join the crowd at the palace gates.

Mr Apple and Dusty Dogwood headed the procession, lanterns held high.

> *"Roast the chestnuts, heat the wine,*
> *Pass the cups along the line,*
> *Gather round, the log burns bright,*
> *It's warm as toast inside tonight,"*

sang the mice as the log came into view.

Teasel, Clover and Catkin were perched on the huge branch and as it was dragged up to the palace gates, Primrose and Wilfred scrambled up behind.

151

The mice pulled the log carefully over the threshold and Basil threw some bramble wine onto the bark. "Merry Midwinter!" he called.

At last the log was here. The midwinter celebrations could begin.

A fire had been laid ready in the hearth of the Great Hall and the log was rolled onto it. Everyone was handed a cup of steaming punch. Old Mrs Eyebright was to light the fire, and she held up a burning taper.

"To Summer!" she announced and Mr Apple stooped to help her thrust the taper into the fire.

"To Summer!" echoed the mice.

The bright flames licked the mossy bark and soon the log was ablaze. The mice helped themselves to supper

which was spread on a table near the fire and Basil
refilled their cups.

"Why don't you take off your cloak, dear?" said
Lady Woodmouse. "It's very hot here by the fire."

"Not just yet, Mama," said Primrose. "I'm still a
bit chilly."

When they had eaten
all they could, they
drew their chairs up
round the hearth and the
entertainment began. Mr Apple made huge shadows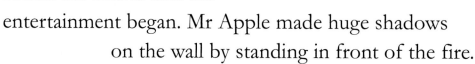
on the wall by standing in front of the fire.
He made the shape of a weasel with a
mean little eye, and a snake's head,
a fox, and with the aid of a curtain,
a bat. The little mice squealed and
laughed. Next, Basil played a jig on
his fiddle and Dusty did some conjuring
tricks. Then they tried to pass a crabapple
right round the circle, holding it under
their chins, and after that
Lord Woodmouse told stirring tales
of olden times. Primrose and Wilfred
nudged each other.

Everyone did a turn until at last Lord Woodmouse said, "And now Primrose, what have you got for us?"

The children jumped up and took their places in front of the fire. Drawing their cloaks closely round them, they began:

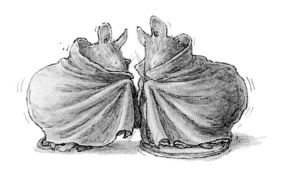

MIDWINTER

When the days are the shortest, the nights are the coldest,
The frost is the sharpest, the year is the oldest,
The sun is the weakest, the wind is the hardest,
The snow is the deepest, the skies are the darkest,
Then polish your whiskers and tidy your nest,
And dress in your richest and finest and best...

For winter has brought you the worst it can bring,
And now it will give you
The promise of SPRING!

Primrose and Wilfred threw off their cloaks and donned

their hats with a flourish. The audience gasped to see
the beautiful clothes which sparkled in the firelight, and
then clapped and cheered louder than ever. The applause
went on for so long that Lord Woodmouse had to ask
them to do it all over again.

At last, Primrose and Wilfred went back to their seats.

"That was wonderful!" whispered Lady Woodmouse, hugging her. "*Wherever* did you find those beautiful clothes?"

Primrose glanced quickly at Wilfred. "In the attic," she mumbled, hoping that her mother would not ask any more awkward questions. Luckily, at that moment, Basil started to tell one last story and everyone settled down to listen.

Primrose and Wilfred gazed at the fire and thought of all the lovely games they would play in their house at the top of the secret staircase. Soon their heads began to nod and in no time at all, they were both fast asleep.

THE HIGH HILLS

It was the very end of autumn. The weather was damp and chilly and Wilfred was spending the day inside with the weavers. *Clickety, clack* went the loom, *whirr, whirr* went the spinning wheel. Lily and Flax were in a hurry.

"We must finish in time," said Flax. "We promised Mr Apple."

"What are you making?" asked Wilfred.

"Blankets," replied Lily.

"Who are they for?" said Wilfred.

"They are for the voles in the High Hills," replied Flax. "They have just discovered that the moths have eaten all their quilts and they've no time to make new ones before the cold weather comes. They're too busy gathering stores for winter. We're helping out."

"Can I help too?" asked Wilfred.

"That's kind of you, Wilfred, but not just now," said Lily. "Why don't you find yourself a book to read while I finish spinning this wool?"

Wilfred went over to the bookcase. On a shelf, tucked between volumes on dyestuffs and weaves, he found a thick book called *Daring Explorers of Old Hedge Days*. He settled himself comfortably and began to turn the pages.

"Sir Hogweed Horehound," he read, "determined to conquer the highest peak of the High Hills, for there, he knew, he would discover gold. Alone he set forth, taking in his trusty pack all he needed to survive the rigorous journey. . ."

Wilfred sat entranced. The whirr of the spinning wheel became the swish of eagles' wings, the clatter of the loom, the sound of falling rock, and the drops of rain on the window, jewels from the depths of some forgotten cave. Was there really gold in the hills beyond Brambly Hedge, he wondered.

Suddenly a door slammed. It was his mother come to fetch him home for tea.

"I hope he hasn't been too much trouble," said Mrs Toadflax.

"He has been so quiet, we'd almost forgotten he was here," said Lily. "You can send him down again tomorrow if you like."

Lily and Flax were already hard at work when Wilfred arrived the next morning. He settled down by the window again to read about Sir Hogweed Horehound and his intrepid search for gold.

The morning flew past and by the time Mr Apple arrived to collect Wilfred, Flax and Lily had almost finished the cloth.

"I'm sorry we couldn't match the yellow," said Flax. "We've used the last of Grandpa Blackthorn's lichen and no other dye will do."

"Never mind," said Mr Apple. "It's the blankets they need. We'll take them up to the hills tomorrow."

"The hills," repeated Wilfred. "Are you really going up to the High Hills?"

"Yes," replied Mr Apple. "Why?"

"Can I come?" Wilfred asked desperately. "Please say I can."

"Oh, I don't think so," said Mr Apple. "It's too far. We shall have to stay overnight."

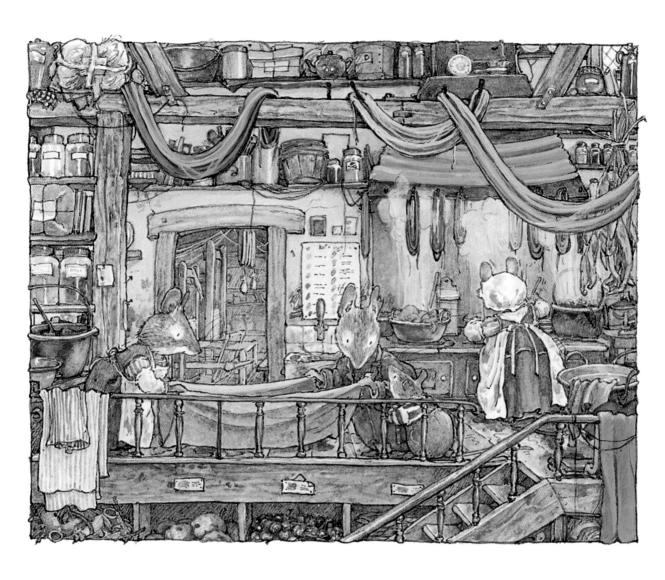

"I'll be very good," urged Wilfred.

Mr Apple relented. "We'll see if your mother
agrees," he said. "Come on, young mouse. It's time
to go home."

To Wilfred's surprise, his mother did agree.

"It will do him good to be in the open air," she said. Wilfred rushed upstairs to pack. He knew just what he would need. Sir Hogweed Horehound had listed all the essential gear in his book: rope, a whistle, food, firesticks, cooking pots, a groundsheet and blankets, a spoon, a water bottle and a first-aid kit.

"And I had better have a special bag for the gold," said Wilfred to himself as he gathered everything together.

He went to bed straight after supper. It was a long way to the High Hills and to get to the Voles' Hole by dusk, they would have to make an early start.

Next morning, soon after dawn, Flax, Lily and Mr Apple called for Wilfred. They were carrying packs on their backs, full of cloth and blankets, and there was honey and cheese and a pudding for the voles from Mrs Apple. Wilfred hurried down the stairs.

"Whatever have you got there?" asked Flax.

"It's my essential gear," explained Wilfred.

"You won't be needing a cooking pot. I've got some sandwiches," said Mr Apple.

"But I must take everything," said Wilfred. His lip began to quiver. "How can I find gold without my equipment?"

"You'll have to carry it then," said Mr Apple. "We can't manage any more."

The first part of the journey was easy. The four mice went up the hedge, past Crabapple Cottage, the Store Stump and Old Oak Palace. Then they rounded the weavers' cottages and arrived at the bank of the stream. Carefully they picked their way over the stepping stones and clambered up into the buttercup meadow.

Wilfred strode through the grass, occasionally lifting his paw to gaze at the distant peaks. Beyond the bluebell woods he could see the path begin to climb.

Mr Apple looked back. "How's my young explorer?" he said. "Ready for lunch?"

"Oh, please," said Wilfred, easing off his pack with relief.

The mice ate their picnic and enjoyed the late autumn sunshine but soon it was time to go on. All through the afternoon they walked. The path became steeper and steeper, and when they looked behind them, they could see the fields and woods and hedges spread out far below.

By tea-time, it was getting dark and cold, and the hills around were shrouded in mist. At last they saw a tiny light shining from a rock beneath an old hawthorn tree.

"Here we are," said Mr Apple. "Knock on the door, Wilfred, will you?"

An elderly vole opened it a crack. When she saw Mr Apple, she cried, "Pip! Fancy you climbing all this way, and with your bad leg too."

"We couldn't leave you without blankets, now could we," said Mr Apple.

The mice crowded into the cottage and were soon sitting round the fire, drinking hot bilberry soup and resting their weary paws.

For Wilfred, the conversation came and went in drifts and soon he was fast asleep. Someone lifted him gently onto a little bracken bed in the corner and the next thing he knew was the delicious smell of breakfast, sizzling on the range.

Wilfred ate heartily, oatcakes with rowanberry jelly, and listened to the voles describing their hard life in the hills. He was disappointed when Mr Apple announced that it was time to leave.

"Can't we explore a bit first?" he begged.

"Flax and I have to get back to work," said Lily, "but why don't you two follow on later?"

"Well," relented Mr Apple, "there are some fine junipers beyond the crag. . ."

"And Mrs Apple *loves* junipers," said Wilfred quickly, "let's get her some."

So the mice said goodbye to the voles and Mr Apple and Wilfred set off up the path.

Wilfred ran on ahead and was soon round the crag. When Mr Apple caught up with him, Wilfred was half way up a steep face of rock.

"Wilfred!" cried Mr Apple. "Come down."

"Just a minute," shouted Wilfred. "I've found something."

Mr Apple watched as Wilfred pulled himself up onto the narrow ledge and started scraping at the rock and stuffing something in his pocket.

"Look!" cried Wilfred. "Gold!"

"Don't be silly, Wilfred," shouted Mr Apple. "That's not gold. Come down at once."

Wilfred looked over the side. His voice faltered. "I can't," he said. "I'm scared."

Mr Apple was exasperated. "Wait there," he shouted. Slowly he climbed the steep rocks, carefully placing his paws in the clefts of the stones. The ledge was very narrow. "We'll edge along this way. Perhaps the two paths

will meet," he said. "We certainly can't go down the way we came up."

As they walked cautiously along the ledge, an ominous mist began to rise from the valley.

"If only we had some rope," said Mr Apple. "We ought to rope ourselves together."

Wilfred put his paw in his pack and produced the rope! Mr Apple tied it carefully round Wilfred's middle

and then round his own. And it was just as well for a few minutes later they were engulfed in a thick white fog.

"Turn to the rock face, Wilfred, we'll ease our way along, one step at a time."

They went on for a long time, then they took a rest. As they sat on the wet rock, the mist parted for a few seconds, just long enough to show a deep strange valley below.

Mr Apple was worried. He had no idea where they were. It looked as though they would have to spend the night on the mountain. It would be very cold and dark, and all he had in his pocket were two sandwiches the voles had given him for the journey down. His leg was feeling stiff and sore too. What was to be done? He explained the situation to Wilfred.

"It's all my fault," said Wilfred, "I didn't mean us to get lost. I just wanted to find gold like Sir Hogweed."

"Never mind," said Mr Apple. "We must look for somewhere to spend the night."

A short way along the path, the ledge became a little wider. Under an overhang of rock a small cave ran back into the mountainside.

"Look," cried Wilfred, slinging his pack inside. "Base camp!"

Mr Apple sat gingerly on the damp moss at the mouth of the cave. Everything felt damp, his clothes, his whiskers, his handkerchief.

"I wish I'd brought my pipe, we could have made a fire," he sighed. "Never mind, we'll huddle close and try to keep warm."

But Wilfred was busily searching in his pack again. Out came the firesticks and the tinderbox. "I'll see if there's some dry wood at the back of the cave," he said enthusiastically.

"Wilfred," cried Mr Apple in admiration, "you're a real explorer."

Soon they had a cheerful blaze on the ledge outside the cave. Wilfred produced two blankets and the mice wrapped themselves up snugly while their clothes dried in front of the fire. The little kettle was filled from the water bottle and proudly Wilfred set out a feast of bread and cheese and honeycakes.

"You know," said Mr Apple, as he settled back against the rock, "I haven't enjoyed a meal so much for years."

To while away the time, Mr Apple began to tell Wilfred stories of his adventurous youth, and as they talked, the mists gradually cleared and a starry sky spread out above them. All was quiet but for the murmur of a stream which ran through the valley below like a silver ribbon in the moonlight. Warmed by the fire, they became drowsy and soon fell asleep.

The next morning they were woken by the sun shining into the cave.

"It's a beautiful day," called Wilfred, peering over the ledge, "and I can see a path down the mountain."

Mr Apple sat up and stretched his leg. It still hurt. "We'll have to go down slowly, I'm afraid," he said.

"Is it your leg?" said Wilfred. "I can help," and he brought out a jar of comfrey ointment from his first-aid kit.

They packed up and set off down the path. Mr Apple did the best he could but his leg was very painful. He managed to get as far as the stream but then he stopped and sat on a boulder with a sigh. "I can't go any further," he said. "What are we to do?"

The two mice sat in silence and watched the water swirl past the bank.

"Don't worry," said Wilfred, trying to be cheerful. "We'll think of something."

Suddenly he jumped up. "I've got it," he cried excitedly. "We'll *sail* down the stream!" He ran to the bank and with his ice-axe, he hooked out some large sticks that had caught behind a rock in the water. Using his rope to lash them together, he made a raft. "Come on," said Wilfred, "we'll shoot the rapids!"

"Are you sure this is a good idea?" said Mr Apple. "Wherever will we end up?"

"Don't worry," said Wilfred. "It's all going to be all right."

Carefully they climbed onto the raft, Mr Apple let go of the bank and they were off!

They were swept to the middle of the stream as it raced down the mountainside, twisting and turning, sweeping and splashing, careering over rocks and cutting through deep banks.

"My hat," shouted Wilfred. "I've lost my hat."

"Never mind that," cried Mr Apple, "just hold on tight. There's a boulder ahead."

Wilfred gripped the sides of the raft, and somehow they managed to keep the raft, and themselves, afloat.

Down by the stream, Dusty was ferrying a search party of mice over to the buttercup meadows when he suddenly caught sight of a small red hat floating along on the current.

"Look there," he shouted. All the mice peered over the side of the boat.

"It's Wilfred's hat," cried out Mrs Toadflax. "Whatever can have happened to him?"

"Can he swim?" asked Mrs Apple anxiously.

Meanwhile Wilfred and Mr Apple were beginning to enjoy their trip on the river. The ground had levelled out and the pace of the stream had become gentler. They looked about them with interest.

"Wilfred," called Mr Apple, "can you see what I can see? I'm sure that's our willow ahead."

Wilfred stared at the bank. "It is!" he yelled.

"And there's the Old Oak Palace and the hornbeam. This is *our* stream!"

As they rounded the bend, they saw the Brambly Hedge mice climbing out of Dusty's boat. At the very same moment, Mrs Apple looked up and cried, "Look! Look! There they are!"

The mice turned in amazement; the raft was almost abreast of them.

"Quick," shouted Dusty, "catch hold of this rope and I'll haul you to shore."

As the two mice clambered out of the raft and up onto the bank, they all hugged each other.

"Wilfred, you're safe," cried Mrs Toadflax.

"My dear, what has happened to your leg?" said Mrs Apple.

Lord Woodmouse took charge. "Come on, everybody," he said. "Let's get these travellers home and dry, and then we can hear the full story."

The mice made their way along the hedgerow to the hornbeam tree. Soon everybody was sitting round the fire, eating cake and drinking acorn coffee.

"Now tell us exactly what happened," urged Flax.

"Well, it was my fault," explained Wilfred again. "I was looking for gold and I got stuck. Mr Apple had to rescue me and then we got lost. And Mr Apple's leg hurt so much, we had to come back on the raft."

"Did you find any gold?" interrupted Primrose.

"No, only this silly old dust," said Wilfred, pulling the bag out of his pocket. Flax and Lily gasped.

"Wilfred! That's not dust. That's Grandpa Blackthorn's lichen. It's very rare. You *are* clever! Wherever did you find it?"

Primrose ran to fetch some paper and Wilfred proudly drew a map so that they could find the place again.

"And when we go, you shall come with us, Wilfred," promised Lily.

Mr Apple was tired and soon he and Mrs Apple went home to Crabapple Cottage. One by one, the visitors drifted away. It was time for the explorer to go to bed.

Wilfred followed his mother up the stairs.

"What adventures!" she said, washing his face and paws and helping him take off his muddy dungarees.

Wilfred climbed into bed. As his mother tucked him in, he thought of his night beneath the stars and snuggling down under his warm blankets, he was soon fast asleep.

SEA STORY

Primrose woke early that summer morning. She dressed quickly and tiptoed down to the kitchen. Her mother was already up, packing a rain cloak and hat into a small bag.

"Off you go," she said. "Take this apple to eat on the way. We'll see you later to say goodbye."

Outside the sun was already warm, and a light breeze stirred the leaves and branches of Brambly Hedge.

"Perfect," said Primrose, "just right for an adventure."

She ran across the field, through the long grass and down to the stream. There she found Dusty, Poppy and Wilfred hard at work, loading provisions on to Dusty's boat.

"Here you are at last," said Dusty. "I was beginning to think we'd have to leave you behind."

Wilfred helped Primrose carry her bag down the steep wooden steps to the cabin below.

"Look at this!" he said, pointing to an ancient yellow map spread out on the chart table.

"Does it show where we're going?" she asked.

"Yes," said Dusty, "it's the old Salters' map. Here's our hedge, and we've got to sail all the way down this river," he pointed to a wiggly blue line, "to the sea!"

On the bank a small crowd of mice had gathered to see them off.

"Will they be all right?" asked Mrs Apple anxiously. "Dusty's never sailed so far before."

"Look, my dear," said Mr Apple, "if the sea mice can manage to get the salt all the way up to us, I'm sure Dusty can sail downstream to fetch it."

"I can't think why we've run out," said Mrs Apple. "It's never happened before. Perhaps I shouldn't have salted all those walnuts."

"Stop worrying," said Mr Apple. "Look, they're about to leave."

"All aboard?" called Dusty. He hoisted the sail, cast off and turned the *Periwinkle* into the current. The voyage was about to begin.

The fresh breeze took them quickly downstream.
Primrose and Wilfred stood by the rail and waved until
everyone was out of sight, and then ran to explore
the boat.

They each chose a bunk, Primrose the top one, Wilfred
the one below, and stowed away their toys and clothes.
Then they hurried back up to help Dusty with the sails.

Poppy prepared a picnic lunch which they ate on deck, watching the trees and riverbanks as they passed by.

"The wind's getting up," said Dusty, as he cleared away, "make sure that everything's secure." At that moment the boat began to heel to one side, and an apple bounced to the floor.

"Can I steer?" Wilfred asked.

"Not in this wind, old chap."

"We're going rather fast," said Poppy.

"Yes, we'll be there in no time," said Dusty cheerfully, hauling in on the ropes.

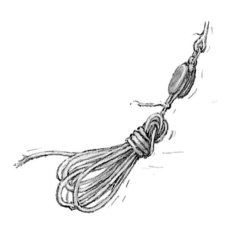

All afternoon the boat sped along, past rushes, trees and fields.

"Look out for a sheltered spot where we can moor up for the night," said Dusty. "I don't like the look of that sky."

"Will this do?" asked Poppy as they rounded a bend in the stream. Dusty turned the *Periwinkle* in towards the bank, and Poppy threw a rope around a twisted root to make it fast.

They were all glad to go below deck to get warm. Poppy lit the lamps, and heated some soup on the stove.

After supper, they sat round the table telling stories and singing songs until it was time for bed. The children, tired after all the fresh air, snuggled happily into their bunks. Outside, the water lapped the sides of the boat, and rocked them gently to sleep.

197

Next morning, Primrose woke to the sound of the wind rushing through the willows on the bank. Poppy was already up, making toast. Dusty and Wilfred were at the chart table, studying the map.

"You'll need to dress warmly today," said Poppy.

Soon the sails were up and they were on their way again. Wilfred helped Dusty on deck, and Primrose looked out for landmarks for Poppy to find on the map.

The day went quickly as the boat skimmed along down the river. By tea time the children had decided to become explorers.

"Look out! Sea Weasels!"
shouted Wilfred.

He jumped into the cockpit,
tripped over a rope, and knocked the
tiller from Dusty's paw. Dusty grabbed for it, but too
late – the boat swung round and headed for the bank.
There was a dreadful scraping noise and the boat
stopped dead. They had run aground.

"We'll *never* get to the sea now," wailed Primrose.
Wilfred hung his head; he felt close to tears.

"Sorry, Dusty," he muttered.

"We won't get off this evening," sighed Dusty, trying
to lever the boat away with an oar. "We'd better go
below and have supper."

The sound of heavy rain greeted the mice next morning. When Dusty looked through the porthole he saw that the water level had risen during the night and floated them clear.

"Hooray," he shouted, and dashed up on deck to take the tiller. "Fetch the map; I think we're nearly there."

Primrose pointed ahead. "Look, that must be Seagull Rock. I can see some boats."

As they drew closer, they saw some water shrews fishing on the bank.

Dusty cupped his paws. "Are we on course for Sandy Bay?" he called.

"Best anchor here and take the path up to the cliffs,"
said the water shrew.

Dusty moored up neatly between the other boats and
the four mice stepped ashore. Slowly they made their
way up the steep path through the pine trees.

At last they stepped up to the very brow of the hill,
and there, spread out before them, glittering in the
afternoon sun, was. . .

. . .the sea.

"It's so big!" gasped Primrose.

"And so blue!" added Wilfred.

One after another, clutching at tufts of marram grass for support, they slithered down the path.

"Which way now?" asked Primrose.

Dusty looked at the map. "To the right," he said, "past the sea campions."

Poppy was the first one to catch sight of a group of mice sitting by a door in the sandy cliffs.

"Excuse me," she called, "we're looking for Purslane Saltapple."

"Well, that's me!" replied one of the mice.

Dusty, delighted, ran to shake his paw. "We're from Brambly Hedge," he explained. "We've run out of salt."

"Then it's a fair wind that blew you here," said Purslane. "Let me introduce my wife Thrift, and our children Pebble, Shell and baby Shrimp."

202

"You must be exhausted," said Thrift. "Come inside, do, and make yourselves comfortable. I expect you'd like to wash your paws."

She led them down a passage to the bathroom. "This is the water for washing," she said, pointing to a pitcher on the floor. "If you'd like a drink, come along to the kitchen."

Poppy and Dusty's bedroom looked straight onto the sea. Primrose and Wilfred were to sleep in the nursery.

Poppy left them to unpack and went to find Thrift.
She was busy in the kitchen, rinsing some brown fronds
in a colander.

"Have you ever tasted seaweed?" she asked.

"No," Poppy replied, "but I'm sure it will be very
interesting to try it."

Soon they were sitting round the table, and trying their first taste of seaside food.

"What's this?" asked Wilfred warily, prodding the pile of vegetables on his plate.

"Marsh samphire, of course," said Pebble.

"Do I have to eat it?" whispered Wilfred.

Poppy coughed and quickly asked, "How long have the Saltapples been here, Purslane?"

"Our family has lived in this dune for generations. A long, long time ago our ancestors left the Green Fields and settled here. We've never been back, and I've often wondered what it's like."

At this, they began to tell each other about their very different lives in the hedgerow and by the sea.

"I've brought you a few things from Brambly Hedge," said Poppy, fetching her basket. Mrs Apple's honeycakes and strawberry jelly tasted strangely sweet to the Sea Mice, and the candied violets had to be put out of the baby's reach.

"Bedtime, children," said Thrift. "If it's fine, we'll go to the beach tomorrow."

As soon as they were up, the children wanted to go straight to the sea.

"You'd better wear sunhats," said Thrift. "It's going to be hot. We'll take a picnic and spend the day there."

While Pebble and Wilfred built a sand palace, Shell and Primrose hunted for treasure in the rock pools, and Shrimp raced along the shore, getting in everyone's way.

The grown-ups spread out the picnic cloth, and reminisced about friends and relations as they watched the children play.

Suddenly, Poppy noticed that the waves were starting to creep up the beach, and she called the children back to the dune.

"It's the tide," explained Purslane. "It goes out and comes in twice every day. Soon the beach will be covered with water. It's time to go home."

On the third day, Wilfred woke to see dark clouds
rolling in over the sea. Purslane hurried past the nursery
door, pulling on his waterproofs.

"I've got to get the salt pans covered before the storm
breaks," he cried. "Come and help!"

They ran through a tunnel to the back of the dune and
out into the rising wind. Purslane paused to hoist up a
red flag, and they scrambled down through the rough
grass to the salt marsh. Wilfred could see two huge dishes
in the ground. One of them was covered and the other
open to the sky.

Purslane ran to release a lever and struggled to push the cover from one dish to the other.

"What's in here?" shouted Wilfred.

"We put seawater in one pan," said Purslane, "the sun dries up the water and leaves the salt for us to collect. The other one is to catch rainwater for us to drink."

Just as they finished lashing down the cover, the rain swept in from the sea. By the time they got home, huge waves were crashing on to the beach, and spray spattered against the windows.

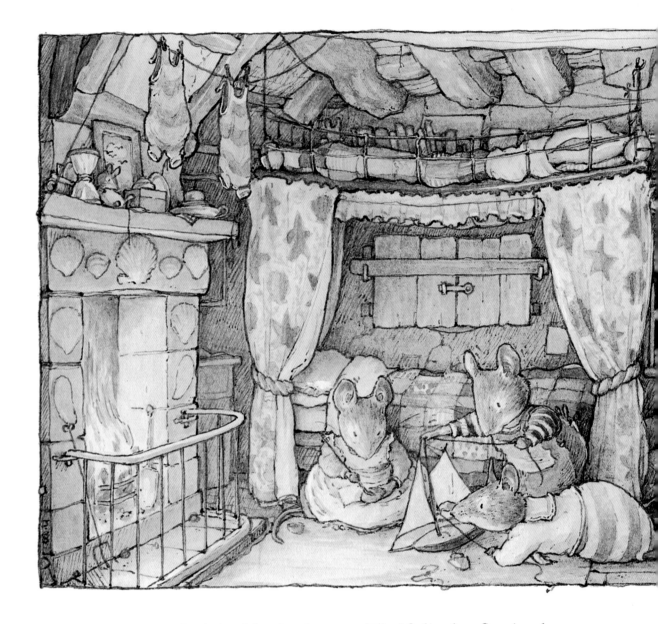

It was dark inside the house. Thrift lit the fire in the
nursery and trimmed the lamp.

"Sometimes we have to stay in for days and days,"
said Shell.

"Especially in the winter," added Pebble.

The children played dominoes and five stones and
made pictures with seaweed.

Pebble helped Wilfred make a little boat with real
sails and rigging, and Primrose painted a beautiful
stone mouse as a present for her mother.

The storm blew itself out in the night. As soon as he got up, Purslane felt the seaweed by the front door and held up his paw to check the wind.

"It's set fair for your journey home," he said.

"Then I think we should be off as soon as we can," said Dusty.

"We must fetch the salt up from the store," said Purslane. "Will three barrels be enough?"

While their parents were busy, the children went off to play hide-and-seek in the maze of tunnels under the dune. They hid in storerooms full of pungent seaweed, behind jars of pickles and roots, and heaps of glistening shells.

"Let's go down to the storm bunker," said Pebble when he had found them all. He led them to some cold dark rooms deep in the heart of the dune.

"We come down here when it gets really rough," said Shell. "It's safer."

"Where are you?" called Thrift faintly. "It's time to leave."

215

Reluctantly, Primrose and Wilfred went to the nursery to collect their things. Wilfred tied his boat to his haversack and put his collection of stones in his pocket. Primrose stood and gazed out of the window. "I don't want to go home," she said.

"We've a present for you," said Pebble quickly. "This is a special shell. Every time you hold it to your ear, you'll hear the sound of the sea and that will remind you to come and see us again."

Dusty and Purslane loaded the barrels of salt on to a handcart, and laden down with luggage and gifts, the little party set off along the dune.

They scrambled down the cliff path to the *Periwinkle* and with some difficulty loaded everything on board.

"Keep that salt dry, mind," said Purslane.

"Try and visit us one day," said Poppy. "We'd like to show you Brambly Hedge."

"All aboard!" called Dusty.

"And no stowaways," added Poppy, lifting Shrimp out of a basket.

They hugged their new friends goodbye, and thanked them for all their help. Poppy loosened the mooring ropes and Dusty hoisted the sail. He steered the boat into the stream once more and Primrose and Wilfred waved until Shell and Pebble were out of sight.

> *"I'm a salter on the salty sea*
> *A' sailing on the foam,*
> *But the salter's life is sweetest*
> *When the sail is set for home,"*

sang Wilfred as a fresh breeze caught the sails and swept them round a bend in the river.

Poppy's Babies

It was the beginning of summer. Outside, the trees were in leaf and sunshine sparkled on the stream. The millwheel turned in the cool shadows of the riverbank and inside the mill Dusty Dogwood was busy grinding the corn for the mice of Brambly Hedge.

Poppy was upstairs trying to persuade her new babies to go to sleep but every time they closed their eyes, the clatter of the mill shook the floorboards and woke them up again.

She opened the door to the stairs and a cloud of flour dust blew into her face.

"Dusty, please finish soon. It's time for the babies' nap."

"I'll do my best," he called back.

The babies were still awake when two visitors peeped round the door.

"Do you know that there are ninety-two stairs up to your kitchen?" gasped Primrose.

"However do you manage with the babies?" asked Lady Woodmouse, giving Poppy a kiss.

"It's very difficult," Poppy replied. She looked as though she was about to cry.

"How sweet they are," said Lady Woodmouse. "This one looks just like Dusty."

"That's Rose. Here is Buttercup, and the little one is Pipkin."

"I can't wait for their Naming Day," said Primrose. "When is it?"

"Just two days away!" said Lady Woodmouse.

At last the millwheels stopped turning and the babies slept. The visitors tiptoed out and Poppy sat down to rest. She was exhausted.

Dusty bagged up the flour and went over to the Store Stump. He found Mr Apple sitting at his workshop door, putting the finishing touches to a wooden mouse on wheels.

Wilfred, who was meant to be helping, was finding it much more amusing to play in the wood shavings.

"Hello, Dusty," said Mr Apple. "How are those babies of yours?"

"Noisy," laughed Dusty, "but great fun. Poppy is not so happy though. The mill is a very inconvenient place to live. It's noisy, dusty and damp and has far too many stairs."

"Come and live at our house," offered Wilfred.
"My mother loves babies."

"Thank you, Wilfred, but I fancy your mother has
enough on her hands with the four of you."

"I wonder what we can do to help Poppy," said
Mr Apple sympathetically.

Dusty returned later in the day to collect some wood for a repair to the mill.

"Come with me," said Mr Apple. Dusty and Wilfred followed him to a little cottage in a hawthorn tree next to the Store Stump.

"I've never noticed this house before," said Dusty.

"It's been empty for years. I use it to keep my timber dry," said Mr Apple.

While Dusty chose a suitable plank, Wilfred peered at an old cooking range.

"Does this still work?" he asked.

"I expect so," said Mr Apple. "It used to be very cosy when my aunt lived here." Suddenly he raised a paw. "Dusty, Wilfred has given me an idea. Suppose we clean the cottage and paint it. Would it suit you and Poppy?"

Dusty thought for a moment and then he said excitedly, "You know, I think it might!"

"Poppy would love this," Dusty said, looking at a
small sunny room. "It's just the right size for a nursery."

"Let's get everything ready for Naming Day," said
Mr Apple. "Do you think we can keep it a secret?"
He looked pointedly at Wilfred.

"I won't say anything," said Wilfred. "Promise."

Mr Apple and Wilfred
went off to Crabapple Cottage
to tell Mrs Apple about the plan and Dusty hurried
home to help give the babies their bath.

"Look," cried Poppy.
"Buttercup's learnt to crawl."
Dusty lifted her up and
gave her a hug.

"I do wish we lived somewhere else," said Poppy.
"I have to watch them every minute of the day."

Mrs Apple had alerted all the mice along the hedge and early next morning they began to arrive at Mayblossom Cottage with buckets and brooms. The windows were opened wide and the floors swept, sanded and scrubbed. Mrs Apple wiped down the dresser shelves and cleaned out the cupboards and Mrs Toadflax polished the bath. Dusty lit a pile of twigs in each grate to check that the chimneys weren't blocked.

"Now for the whitewash," said Mr Apple. "Do you want to mix it, Wilfred?"

"As soon as the walls are dry, we can start to fetch the furniture from the mill," said Dusty.

"But how can we do that without Poppy seeing?"

"Ah, Mrs Apple's thought of a plan," said Mr Apple.

The next day Lady Woodmouse and Poppy sat under
the hedge, sewing. Bees buzzed in and out of the flowers
in the early morning sunshine and the scent of hawthorn
blossom filled the air.

"There, that quilt's finished," said Lady Woodmouse, putting the last stitch into a yellow flower.

"I've still got Pipkin's gown to make," sighed Poppy. "However am I going to finish it in time?"

"We've had a good idea," said Lady Woodmouse. "Why don't you all come and stay at the Palace with us tonight. We can work on the gowns together and Primrose can help you to dress the babies for Naming Day tomorrow morning."

"That would help Dusty too," said Poppy. "He seems to be very busy at the moment."

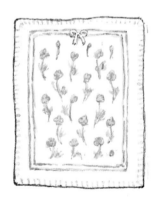  

By late that afternoon, the cottage was almost ready.
Wilfred put a last coat of whitewash on the nursery walls
and Dusty measured up for the furniture.

"There, everything fits," he said with satisfaction.
"Let's go back to the mill for tea."

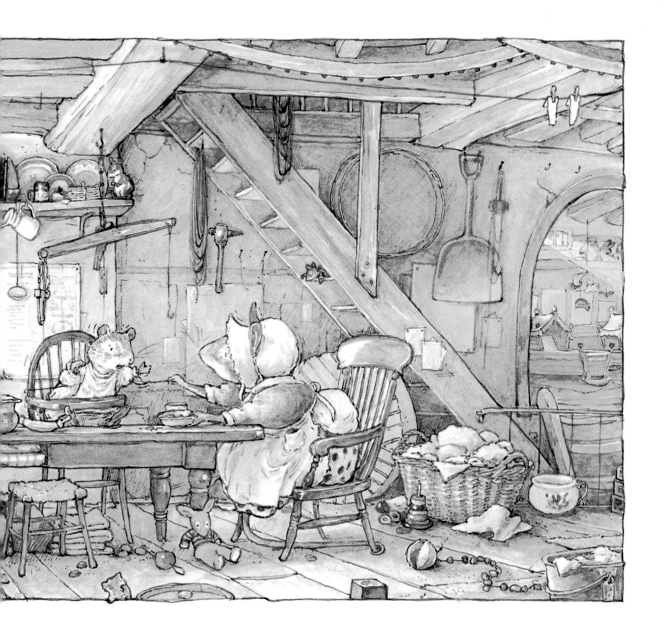

"Goodness, whatever have you two been doing?"
asked Poppy, staring at Wilfred's fur.

"Painting," said Wilfred proudly. "I mean. . ."

"Something for the babies," said Dusty quickly.

"You are a kind mouse, Wilfred," said Poppy.

Up and down Brambly Hedge, the mice were all busy. In the Palace kitchen, Mrs Crustybread was making a special cake and her daughter Cicely made rosepetal butter and creamy junket.

Over at Mayblossom Cottage, Mrs Toadflax had laid the table and was now hanging curtains, while up in the nursery, Lady Woodmouse unpacked the three little quilts.

"We're ready to fetch Poppy now," she said.

"Right," said Dusty. "As soon as you're at the Palace, we'll start to move in the furniture."

Down at the mill, Poppy was busy packing.

"There seems to be so much to take," she said, folding up three little nightgowns. "Perhaps I should stay here after all."

"No, no," said Lady Woodmouse hastily. "Primrose will be so disappointed if you don't come."

Eventually, they managed to get the nappies, bottles, toys, prams and babies down the stairs (all ninety-two of them!) and were ready to set off to the Palace.

The babies loved the journey. Rose gurgled when she
saw the stream, Pipkin threw his rattle in the water and
when they reached the field, Buttercup tried to get out
of the pram.

At the door of Old Oak Palace, Dusty kissed his family goodnight.

"Don't wait up for me," he said, "I've one or two things to sort out before tomorrow."

The babies were bathed and put into their nightgowns. They were so excited by their new surroundings that they didn't want to settle but at last they all fell asleep in the quiet of the hedgerow evening.

Lady Woodmouse lit the lamp, then she and Poppy sat and stitched the last of the lace on to the babies' gowns.

"How peaceful it is here," said Poppy.

As she spoke, a curious squeaking, bumping noise came through the open window.

"Whatever is that?" Poppy asked, startled.

Lady Woodmouse got up quickly and drew the curtains.

"Just Lord Woodmouse tidying up," she said. "We'd better get to bed. We'll need to be up before first light tomorrow."

Very early next morning, all the mice gathered
beneath the hawthorns for the Naming Ceremony.
As dawn broke, Poppy handed Old Vole the first baby.
Primrose held up a cup of dew, freshly gathered from
the flowers, for Old Vole to sprinkle on the baby's head.

"The buds on the branches blossom and flower,
The blackbirds sing in the leafy bower,
And over the hill comes the rising sun,
To shine on the fields, and on you, little one."

"We name you Rose," said Old Vole, gently.

Just as Old Vole named the last baby Pipkin, the mice heard the patter of raindrops on the leaves.

"Oh dear, we'll all get wet," cried Poppy.

"No, no. Come this way," said Lady Woodmouse. "Bring the babies."

Poppy and Dusty ran towards the Store Stump and Dusty stood aside to let Poppy take shelter in the open door of a cottage.

Poppy found herself in the kitchen. Bright china that looked rather familiar was arranged on the dresser shelves and garlands of flowers hung from newly washed beams.

"What a dear little house," said Poppy.

"Let's look round," said Dusty.

Leaving Primrose in charge of the babies, Poppy and Dusty climbed the stairs.

"It's so cosy," she said as they reached the landing.
"I wonder who lives here?"

Dusty led her to a small room that was warm and
bright. Fresh curtains hung at the windows and
beneath them stood three little cots, each with its
own embroidered quilt. One was pink, one was yellow
and one was blue.

"But Dusty. . ." she cried.

"Yes," said Dusty, "with love from all your friends in Brambly Hedge. Welcome home!"

Poppy threw her paws round Dusty.

"This is the nicest surprise I've ever had," she said, then she ran downstairs to thank each mouse in turn.

"It's time to cut the cake!" shouted Wilfred.

Everyone was given a large slice and Basil served a summer punch with flowers floating on top. There were cowslip and violet salads, rosepetal sandwiches, primrose pottage and meadowsweet tea.

The babies crawled around underfoot and Poppy was glad of Mr Apple's gates on the stairs. Then they were given some cake and got very sticky. Soon Rose began to cry, followed by Buttercup, and Pipkin rolled under the table.

"Poor babies, you're tired," said Poppy. "I'm going to put you into your cots."

The baby mice snuggled under their new quilts and by the time Poppy bent to kiss them, they were fast asleep. She tiptoed back downstairs to join the guests in the kitchen.

Mr Apple proposed a toast.

"To the babies," he whispered, "and their new home."

"To Rose, Buttercup and Pipkin," added Mrs Apple. "Bless their little whiskers."